This book is for Peregrines class at
Gastrells Community Primary School, 2017.
Thank you all for your great pictures!

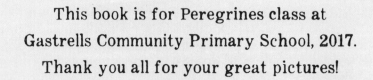

BLOOMSBURY CHILDREN'S BOOKS
Bloomsbury Publishing Plc
50 Bedford Square, London, WC1B 3DP, UK
BLOOMSBURY, BLOOMSBURY CHILDREN'S BOOKS and the Diana logo are trademarks of Bloomsbury Publishing Plc
First published in Great Britain by Bloomsbury Publishing Plc

Text and illustrations copyright © Tom Percival 2018

Tom Percival has asserted his rights under the Copyright, Designs and Patents Act, 1988, to be identified as the Author/Illustrator of this work

A catalogue record for this book is available from the British Library

ISBN 978 1 4088 9213 8 (HB)
ISBN 978 1 4088 9215 2 (PB)
ISBN 978 1 4088 9214 5 (eBook)

1 3 5 7 9 10 8 6 4 2

Printed and bound in China by Leo Paper Products, Heshan, Guangdong
All papers used by Bloomsbury Publishing Plc are natural, recyclable products from wood grown in well managed forests.
The manufacturing processes conform to the environmental regulations of the country of origin.

To find out more about our authors and books visit www.bloomsbury.com and sign up for our newsletters

Ruby loved being
Ruby.

RUBY'S WORRY

TOM PERCIVAL

BLOOMSBURY
CHILDREN'S BOOKS
LONDON   OXFORD   NEW YORK   NEW DELHI   SYDNEY

She loved to swing up high . . .

and she loved to explore
wild, faraway places.

Sometimes she even went all the way
to the very bottom of the garden!

Ruby was perfectly happy.
Until one day . . .

she discovered

a Worry.

It wasn't a very
big Worry...

In fact, it was so small that, at first,
Ruby hardly noticed it.

But then the Worry
started to grow.

Each day it got a little bit bigger . . .

It just wouldn't
leave her alone.

It was there at breakfast, staring at
her over the cereal box.

And it was STILL there at night,
when she cleaned her teeth.

The funny thing was that no one else could see
Ruby's Worry – not even her teacher.

So Ruby pretended that *she* couldn't see it either.

She *tried* to carry on as if everything was normal – but it just wasn't!

The Worry was *always* there – stopping her
from doing the things that she loved.

Ruby wondered if the Worry
would ever go away.

What if it didn't?

What if it stayed with her *forever*?

Ruby didn't realise, but she was doing the worst
thing you can ever do with a Worry . . .

she was worrying about it!

Now the Worry was
ENORMOUS!

It could barely fit in the kitchen at teatime.

It filled up half of the school bus . . .

and it took up whole rows at the cinema.

The Worry became the only thing that Ruby could think about, and it seemed like she would never feel happy again.

Then, one day, something
unexpected happened . . .

Ruby noticed a boy sitting alone at the park.
He looked how she felt – sad.

And then she noticed something else, something
hovering next to him. Could it be . . .

a Worry?

She asked the boy what was on his mind
and, as he told her, the strangest
thing happened . . .

his Worry began to shrink!

Then Ruby did the best thing you can
ever do if you have a Worry . . .

she talked about it.

As the words tumbled out, Ruby's Worry began to shrink until it was barely there at all.

Soon, both of their Worries were gone!

Finally, Ruby felt like herself again!

Of course, that wasn't the last time that
she ever had a Worry (everyone gets
them from time to time).

But now that she knew how to
get rid of them . . .

they never hung around for long.